CAMP ROCK

Hit the High Notes

Based on "Camp Rock," Written by Karin Hicks & Regina Hicks and Julie Brown & Paul Brown

DISNEY PRESS

New York

Text by Nicole Tocco
The recipes on page 25 were reprinted by permission from *FamilyFun* magazine.

First Edition
1 3 5 7 9 10 8 6 4 2
Library of Congress Catalog Card Number: 2007909631
ISBN 978-1-4231-1608-0

For more Disney Press fun, visit www.disneybooks.com
Visit DisneyChannel.com

Summer is supposed to rock. Duh! But my summer not only rocked, it totally rolled! I got to go to Camp Rock—<u>the</u> place to be if you want anything to do with singing, songwriting, producing, or performing! For a while I didn't think I was going to get my chance to shine, but camp was full of surprises. Sure, there were some not-so-stellar moments (hey, everyone makes a mistake—or two), but they were all worth it. I got to meet so many amazing people, like Shane Gray (total pop-star hottie), my new BFF, Caitlyn Gellar, and Tess Tyler (diva alert!). With all the fun, I figured it would be mean not to share, so here are all the high notes (and some of the low ones) from my Camp Rock summer!

Enjoy and rock on!

—Mitchie

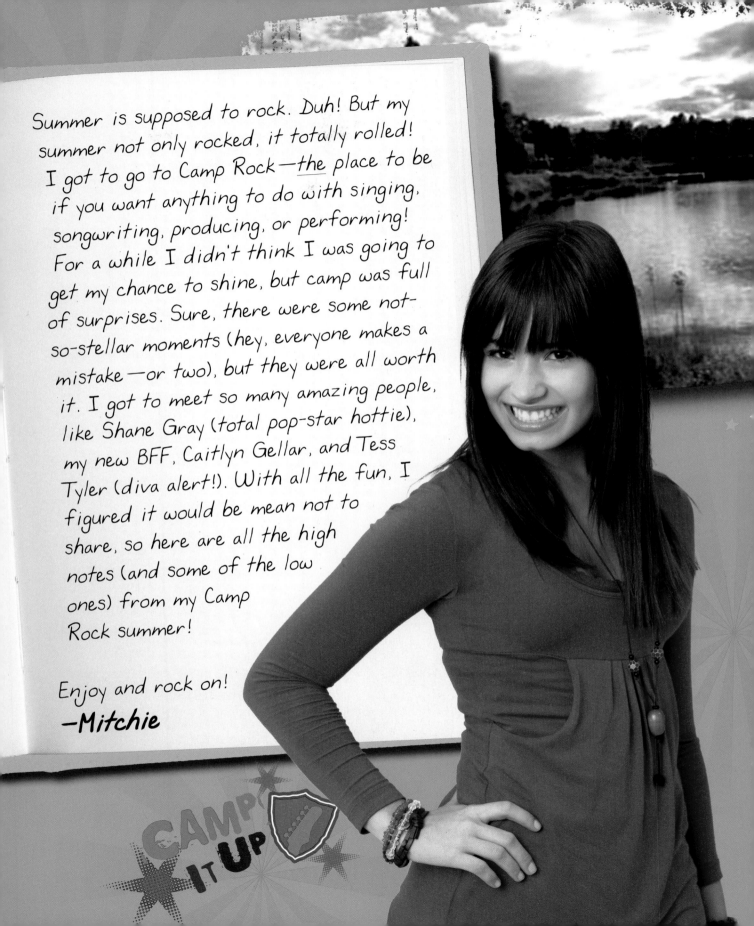

MITCHIE TORRES

I'm Mitchie, and there is one thing I love more than anything—music. It's my life! So, you can imagine how bummed I was when my parents told me they wouldn't be able to send me to Camp Rock. I mean, I gave them a bazillion hints. There were brochures for the camp ALL over the house—in the fridge, behind the sofa, on top of the TV! I couldn't have made it more obvious. None of it mattered, though. It looked like I was going to spend the summer serving burgers at Barney's, a restaurant in my hometown.

But then my parents gave me the best surprise of my life—Mom got a gig as the cook at Camp Rock! Which meant . . . I got to go! Sure, it meant I had to help her out in the kitchen, but how hard could that be?

Turns out the hard part wasn't the helping, it was the acting! See, when I got to camp, I realized that everyone there was rich or had famous parents. So I, sort of, maybe, told everyone that my mom was president of Hot Tunes TV . . . in China.

I know! Not my best moment. AND, I got caught! It took a lot of explaining, but my friends finally forgave me and I got the confidence boost I needed to perform in front of an audience. It turns out that being true to yourself is the best way to rock!

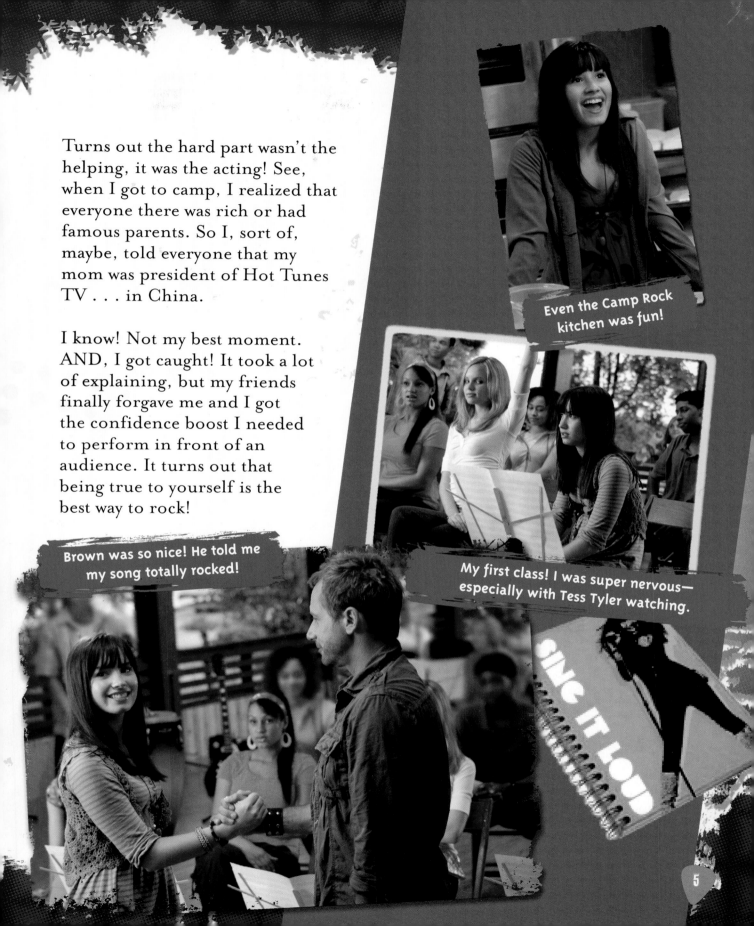

Even the Camp Rock kitchen was fun!

My first class! I was super nervous—especially with Tess Tyler watching.

Brown was so nice! He told me my song totally rocked!

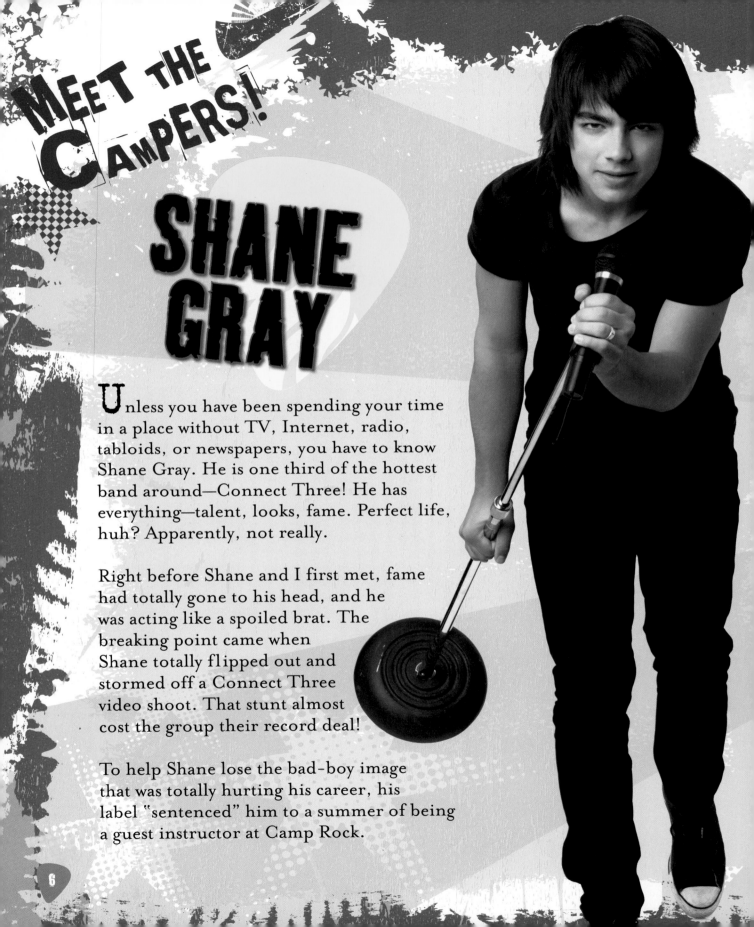

SHANE GRAY

Unless you have been spending your time in a place without TV, Internet, radio, tabloids, or newspapers, you have to know Shane Gray. He is one third of the hottest band around—Connect Three! He has everything—talent, looks, fame. Perfect life, huh? Apparently, not really.

Right before Shane and I first met, fame had totally gone to his head, and he was acting like a spoiled brat. The breaking point came when Shane totally flipped out and stormed off a Connect Three video shoot. That stunt almost cost the group their record deal!

To help Shane lose the bad-boy image that was totally hurting his career, his label "sentenced" him to a summer of being a guest instructor at Camp Rock.

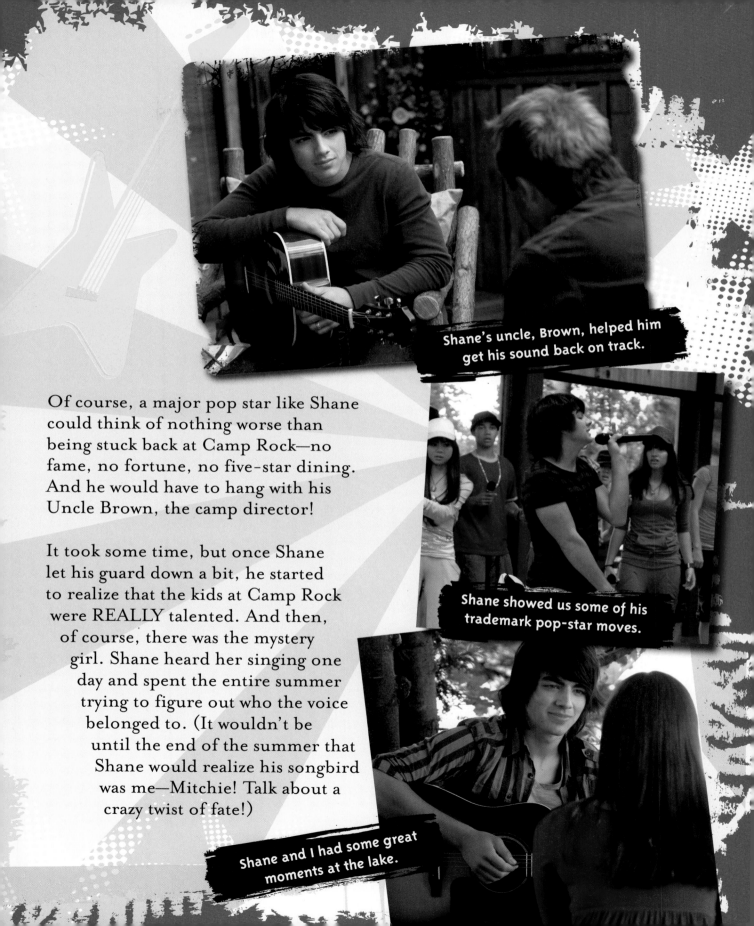

Shane's uncle, Brown, helped him get his sound back on track.

Of course, a major pop star like Shane could think of nothing worse than being stuck back at Camp Rock—no fame, no fortune, no five-star dining. And he would have to hang with his Uncle Brown, the camp director!

It took some time, but once Shane let his guard down a bit, he started to realize that the kids at Camp Rock were REALLY talented. And then, of course, there was the mystery girl. Shane heard her singing one day and spent the entire summer trying to figure out who the voice belonged to. (It wouldn't be until the end of the summer that Shane would realize his songbird was me—Mitchie! Talk about a crazy twist of fate!)

Shane showed us some of his trademark pop-star moves.

Shane and I had some great moments at the lake.

MEET THE CAMPERS!

TESS TYLER

Tess, Tess, Tess—where do I begin? She pretends to be sweet as sugar, but watch out! Tess is THE diva of Camp Rock—and she makes sure everyone knows it.

Tess's mom is the Grammy Award-winning singer T.J. Tyler, which works out well for Tess because she gets awesome concert tickets and really cool stuff to show off. Tess can have anything money can buy. But all she really wants is a little attention from her mom.

Speaking of which, I was SO thrilled when Tess paid attention to me! When she asked me to move into the Vibe

FOLLOW

Cabin with her and Peggy and Ella, I jumped at the chance. Too bad the invite came after I lied about my mom's job.

At first Tess seemed really cool. I got so caught up in being popular, I even let Tess convince me to sing backup. (Not my plan!)

But in the end, I figured out that Tess is just as insecure as the rest of us. So maybe we aren't all that different—but that doesn't mean we are going to be BFFs anytime soon!

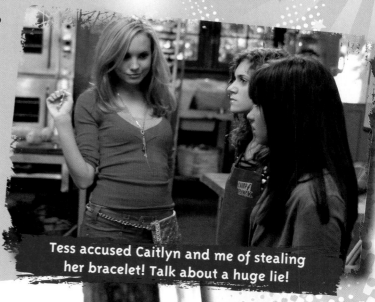

Tess accused Caitlyn and me of stealing her bracelet! Talk about a huge lie!

Tess knew that the key to her success was keeping Peggy and Ella close.

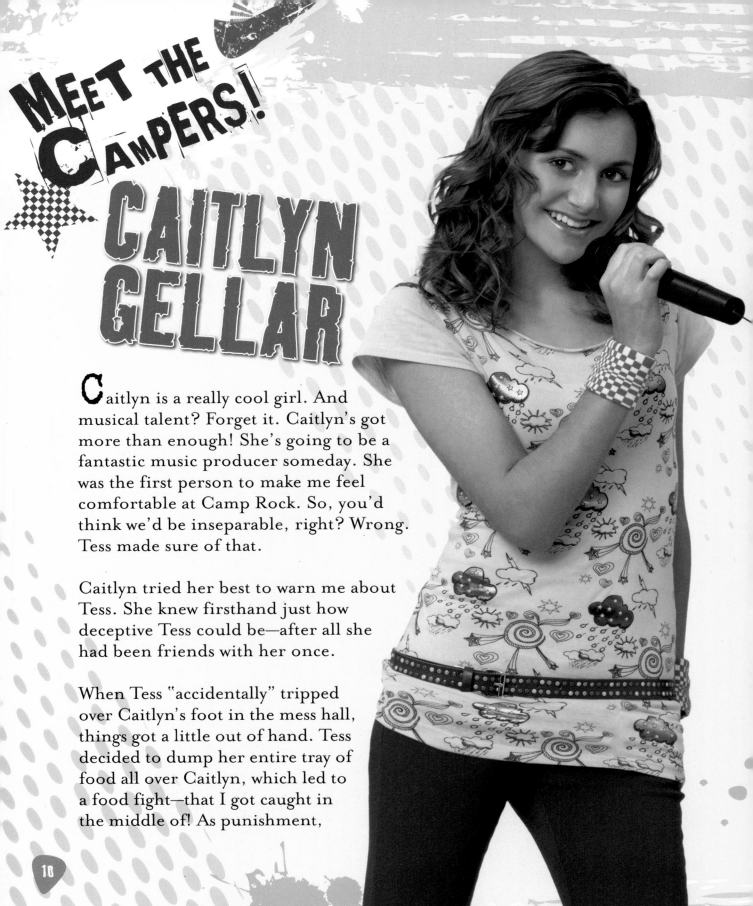

MEET THE CAMPERS!

CAITLYN GELLAR

Caitlyn is a really cool girl. And musical talent? Forget it. Caitlyn's got more than enough! She's going to be a fantastic music producer someday. She was the first person to make me feel comfortable at Camp Rock. So, you'd think we'd be inseparable, right? Wrong. Tess made sure of that.

Caitlyn tried her best to warn me about Tess. She knew firsthand just how deceptive Tess could be—after all she had been friends with her once.

When Tess "accidentally" tripped over Caitlyn's foot in the mess hall, things got a little out of hand. Tess decided to dump her entire tray of food all over Caitlyn, which led to a food fight—that I got caught in the middle of! As punishment,

Brown ended up making Caitlyn work in the kitchen with my mom—and me. Caitlyn just didn't know I'd be there!

I tried to hide my secret from Caitlyn, but she figured it out—she's a pretty smart girl. Despite all that, we ended up becoming really good friends and rocked Final Jam together. I can't wait to hang with her at camp next session!

I discovered tortilla chips aren't fun to clean up!

Camp Rock wasn't all fun and games—it was work sometimes, too!

When Caitlyn gets behind the keyboard—watch out! The girl sure knows how to make a cool sound!

The day Tess told everyone my secret, Caitlyn was so disappointed!

MEET THE CAMPERS!

ELLA

PEGGY

Peggy and Ella are part of Tess's entourage. They are totally different, but they have one thing in common—they love to sing!

Ella doesn't really care about being in the spotlight. Give her some lip gloss and a few bottles of pink nail polish, and she's happy! Don't get me wrong, Ella loves to sing as much as the rest of us, but she doesn't crave the spotlight.

Peggy, on the other hand, always had a solo singing voice—it was just hidden. But at Final Jam, Peggy took the chance and performed solo for the first time. Or should I say, Margaret Dupree took the chance. She completely wowed the entire crowd and ended up winning Final Jam. And that wasn't the best part! Peggy gets to record a duet with Shane Gray and Connect Three!

Ella rocked her own style at Final Jam!

And the winner is . . . Margaret Dupree!

Even Peggy and Ella could get sick of Tess's games.

MEET THE CAMPERS!

The kids at Camp Rock are such cool people—and amazing musicians. When they get together to jam, it's SO cool!

BARRON JAMES
SANDER LOYA

Barron and Sander definitely know how to get the party started and get the crowd going! The two are always creating hot new dance steps that everyone wants to know.

LOLA SCOTT

Lola has a truly amazing voice! Her mom is a star on Broadway and taught her the ropes. When she takes the microphone, watch out!

ANDY

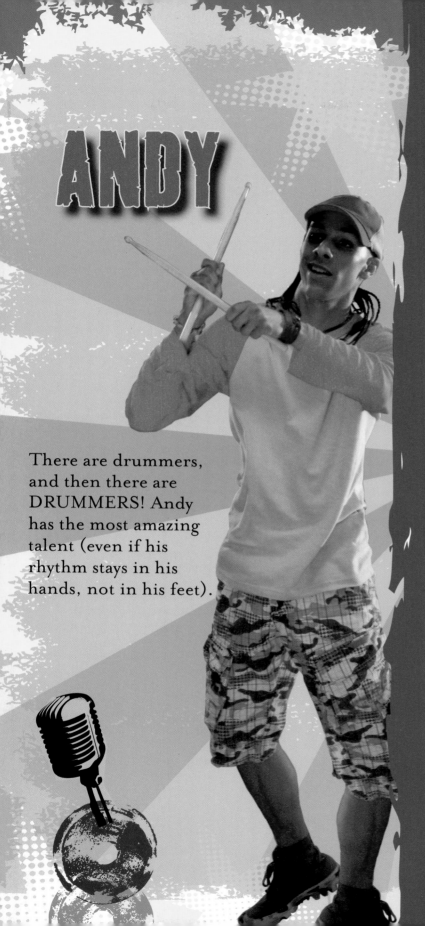

There are drummers, and then there are DRUMMERS! Andy has the most amazing talent (even if his rhythm stays in his hands, not in his feet).

BEATING YOUR OWN DRUM!

Everyone at Camp Rock has very unique musical tastes. What's your musical flavor?

The Rockers: This group knows how to roar on key!

The Goths: The ghostly looks translate to some out-of-this-world sounds!

The Hip-Hop Crowd: Rhythm is just part of the image; beat is everything.

The Country Crooners: Heel-stomping and yeehaws make for a down-home sound.

The Heavy Metal Heads: When their heads start banging, step back!

The Angry-Chick Music Girls: Heartbreak fuels these girls to new musical heights.

CONNIE TORRES

This is my mom, Connie Torres. She and my dad are pretty cool. Mom just started her own business—Connie's Catering—and I have to hand it to her; she did everything she could to send me to Camp Rock, even taking a job as the camp cook!

So while Dad stayed at home to run his hardware store, Mom headed off to Camp Rock with me. She really seemed to enjoy the job, too. I mean, it's not easy cooking for hundreds of kids, but Mom put her heart and soul into it.

Mom has always believed in my talent. And she has always urged me to be me. So she was really disappointed when she found out that I told everyone at camp that she was the president of Hot Tunes TV China. She thought I was embarrassed by her—which I totally wasn't. It took some serious groveling, but she accepted my apology. Phew! That could have made for a bummer end to the summer.

The pasta wasn't the only thing in hot water when Tess accused Caitlyn and me of stealing!

Mom is the best! Even after I lied about her job, she was really there for me.

BROWN CESARIO

Brown is the director of Camp Rock. Along with Dee La Duke, the music director, Brown runs Camp Rock, a job he totally loves. He's a really cool guy, although he's a little prone to name-dropping! He used to play bass guitar for the Wet Crows. He knows just about EVERY musical legend in the industry. (And trust me, he has a story about every one of them!)

Brown is really passionate about music. His motto is "When the music calls, you gotta answer." So, it was really important to him to help his nephew, Shane, to find his voice and get back to making the music he loved. (And if you ask me—and every Connect Three fan out there—he totally succeeded!)

Brown is always giving great advice—even if it comes with a lot of name-dropping!

Fans everywhere should worship Brown—he helped bring Connect Three together!

Brown and Shane had some serious heart-to-hearts early on.

At Final Jam, Brown and Dee ran the show!

CONNECT THREE

Connect Three is a real Camp Rock success story! The guys—Shane, Nate, and Jason—actually connected right here at Camp Rock, and they have been rockin' to the top ever since! They are living proof that, with the right chemistry, ability, and determination, there's no stopping talent!

Connect Three is the HOTTEST group out there! Every girl totally adores the guys, and every guy wants to *be* them! So, you can imagine the excitement when everyone found out that Shane Gray was going to be hanging at Camp Rock this summer (even if he was doing it as payback for his bad-boy ways)! And the noise hit a new level when Brown revealed that all three boys would be judging Final Jam—talk about pressure!

CELEBRITY BLOG

HOME   TV   PHOTOS   K5   FIGHTS   NICE STORIES   STAR CATCHER

CELEB SCANDALS
Bad-boy SHANE GRAY of CONNECT THREE is at it again. Looks like fame has gone right to his head! Just days ago, Shane stormed off the set of Connect Three's latest video after an assistant brought Shane the wrong lunch order(gasp!)! Now Shane has been sentenced to a summer at Camp Rock, the place where he met his bandmates. Can Connect Three survive the aftermath? Or will

star
SCOOP
Volume **14**: Issue: **6**

SPECIAL
CONNECT THREE
COLLECTOR'S
EDITION

WHAT ABOUT
NATE?
what's his idea of
the perfect date?
(READ ON)

the scoop on shane!
are you the girl of his
dreams? take the quiz
and find out!

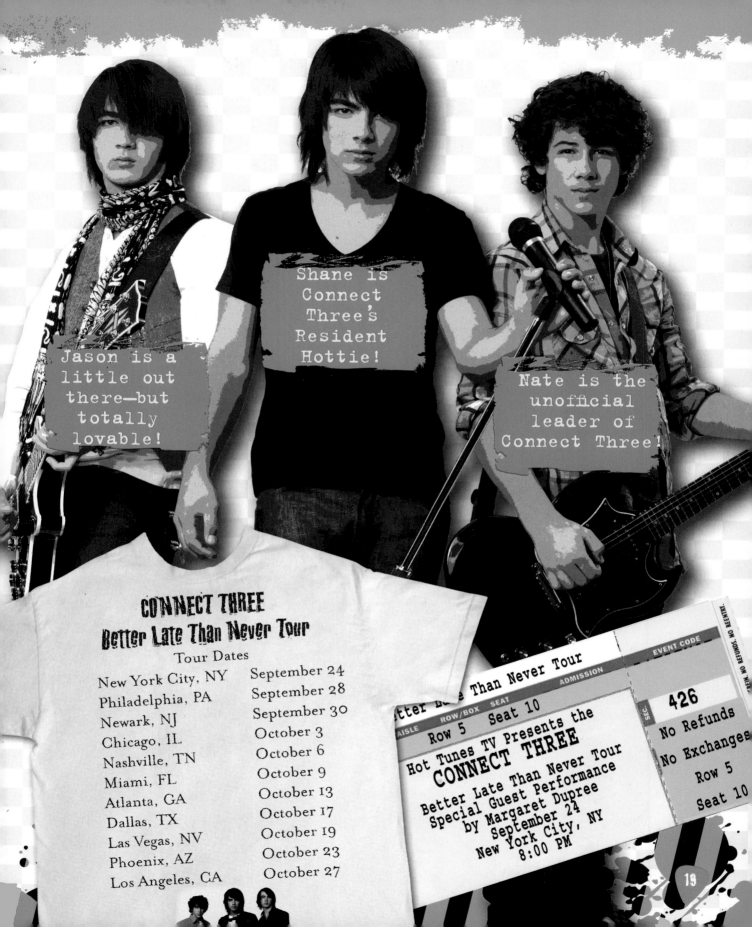

Jason is a little out there—but totally lovable!

Shane is Connect Three's Resident Hottie!

Nate is the unofficial leader of Connect Three!

CONNECT THREE
Better Late Than Never Tour
Tour Dates

New York City, NY	September 24
Philadelphia, PA	September 28
Newark, NJ	September 30
Chicago, IL	October 3
Nashville, TN	October 6
Miami, FL	October 9
Atlanta, GA	October 13
Dallas, TX	October 17
Las Vegas, NV	October 19
Phoenix, AZ	October 23
Los Angeles, CA	October 27

EVENT CODE

etter Late Than Never Tour

ADMISSION

Row 5   Seat 10

SEC. 426

No Refunds
No Exchanges

Row 5

Seat 10

ROW/BOX   SEAT

AISLE

Hot Tunes TV Presents the
CONNECT THREE
Better Late Than Never Tour
Special Guest Performance
by Margaret Dupree
September 24
New York City, NY
8:00 PM

Attention all musicians and music lovers—if you are looking for the ULTIMATE musical experience, Camp Rock is perfect for you! Camp Rock is an awesome place, where you can really express yourself through the supreme channel—MUSIC! So if you see music in your future, whether it's in front of the microphone, behind the camera, or on the keyboard—read on and sign up today! It's sure to be the best summer of your life!

Camp Director:
Brown Cesario

Music Director:
Dee La Duke

SIGN UP TODAY!
Space is limited and filling up fast!

Classes May Include:

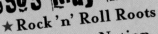

★ Rock 'n' Roll Roots
★ Hip-Hop Nation
★ A Little Bit Country
★ R&B Rhythms
★ Pop-Star Power

...plus many, many more! And at this rockin' camp, you never know who your instructor might be!

CAMP
ROC

The Ultim
Musi
Experi

FAMOUS ALUMNI!

We'll pack your summer with fun, friends, and music!
Enjoy:

Concerts!

Jam Sessions!

Boating!

Swimming!

Campfires!

MITCHIE'S SONGBOOK PART I

I figured that the only way to get a feel for my time at camp is to get an inside peek at what I was thinking. So, here it is. ...Just don't go showing Tess!

True to Me

In a corner the spotlight fades
While I long to shine

Afraid to stand, I do not share
what I have made
The story remains mine

To be kept and held until
another time
When I can raise my voice and
sing along...

True to me.

Camp Rock:
First day
OMG... total freak out! I have never seen so many limos, expensive cells, and designer clothes in one place in my life! Made showing up in the old Connie's Catering truck a real joy. Definitely felt sort of like a fish out of water.

So, not only do these kids have money, but they have oodles of TALENT to go along with it! I always thought I had a pretty decent voice, but when I heard some of these people sing at open mike, I wasn't so sure how good I was anymore. I chickened out... didn't sing at open mike . . . .

OK... so I think I may have messed up—big time. But I had to do SOMETHING. Tess Tyler, total diva of Camp Rock and one of the popular kids, totally talked to me.... I just couldn't tell her that I was kitchen help.... So I told a little white lie... something along the lines of my mom being president of Hot Tunes TV in China. Oh boy, how am I gonna keep this act up all summer?!?

HOTTIE ALERT!!

Shane Gray is at Camp Rock this summer, and he is totally rocking the spoiled star attitude. It makes me kinda mad. I mean, he was totally rude to me in the kitchen and he didn't even know who I was! I've got to say though—he's even cuter in person!!!

Not easy pretending to be someone you're not... not that fun, either. But it is keeping me in with the popular clique. They even asked me to bunk in their cabin and to sing backup with them. So I guess it's worth it... right? We'll see.

MESS HALL MENU

JUST NEED TO FIGURE OUT HOW TO MULTIPLY THE RECIPES SO THEY FEED 300!!

Monday
Breakfast: Rockin' Eggs and Bacon
Lunch: Power-Pop Pizza
Dinner: Rock 'n' Roll Burgers and Fries

(What happened to the World-Famous Torres burgers!?! Dad is going to be bummed!)

Tuesday
Breakfast: Hall of Fame French Toast
Lunch: Soulful Sloppy Joes
Dinner: Sweet Melody Spaghetti and Meatballs

(Cut the French toast into musical note shapes)

Wednesday
Breakfast: Play Me Some Pancakes
Lunch: Tune-in Tuna Salad
Dinner: Chow-Down Chili

(What, Mom? They can't all be musical names!)

Thursday
Breakfast: Opera Omelets
Lunch: Heavy-Metal Mac and Cheese
Dinner: Hip-Hop Tacos

(A fan favorite!)

Friday
Breakfast: Over-the-Top Oatmeal
Lunch: Hip-Hop Taco Surprise
Dinner: Country Western Chicken Nuggets

(Have to use those leftovers!)

Saturday
Breakfast: Excellent As Ever Eggs and Bacon
Lunch: The Song's the Way PB&J
Dinner: Musical Madness Meatloaf

(Now THAT sounds scary!)

Sunday
Breakfast: Bring-It-On Buffet
Lunch: Garage-Band Grilled Cheese
Dinner: Pop-Star Burgers and Fries

(Um, didn't we have these a few days ago when they were Rock 'n' Roll' Burgers and Fries??)

The Song's the Way PB & J

Ingredients:

3 tablespoons peanut butter (crunchy or creamy)
1 whole pita bread
Toppings such as jelly, raisins, grated apples, sliced bananas, Cheerios, and peanuts.

Directions:

1. Spread the peanut butter on the pita bread. Then top with jelly, raisins, Cheerios, grated apples, and/or banana slices. You can arrange the toppings randomly or in a pattern.
2. Use a pizza cutter to slice the pita into wedges. Grip the pizza cutter handle firmly, apply slight pressure, and roll the blade steadily and in a straight line.

ROCKIN' HUMMUS DIP

Ingredients:

1 19-ounce can chickpeas
1 garlic clove
¼ cup tahini
2 to 3 tablespoons lemon juice
2 tablespoons olive oil
¼ teaspoon cumin (optional)

I am, after all, famous for the way I handle my chips! So, here's what I like to dip them in!

Directions:

1. Drain the chickpeas in a colander, then rinse them thoroughly in cold water. Set aside.
2. Peel the garlic clove and place it in a food processor fitted with a metal blade. Process until the garlic is chopped.
3. Add the rinsed chickpeas to the food processor, then add the tahini, lemon juice, olive oil, and cumin, if desired. Process for 1 minute or until smooth.

HEAVY METAL MAC AND CHEESE

Ingredients:

1 pound elbow macaroni
Butter for greasing the dish
3 cups half-and-half
12 to 18 slices American or cheddar cheese
12 Ritz crackers
Salt, pepper, and paprika to taste

Directions:

1. Bring a pot of lightly salted water to a boil. Add the macaroni and cook until tender but still firm. Drain well.
2. Meanwhile, heat the oven to 350 degrees and grease a 13-by-9-inch baking pan or a large casserole dish.
3. Spoon a third of the pasta into the pan, then pour in 1 cup of the half-and-half and cover it all with 4 to 6 slices of cheese. Add two more layers of pasta, half-and-half, and cheese.
4. Place the crackers in a ziplock bag and crush. Add the salt, pepper, and paprika, then sprinkle the crumbs on top of the pasta and cheese. Bake until bubbly, about 30 to 40 minutes.

How To Become A Pop Star:
Top Five Tips From Tess Tyler

Camp Rock really has so much to offer. Check out what the other campers have to say on everything from decorating to stardom.
— Mitchie

Hi, I'm Tess Tyler, but I am sure you knew THAT! I already rule Camp Rock, so it only makes sense for yours truly to teach you how to make it to the top. If you're serious about becoming a pop princess, pay attention!

Tip #5
Never, EVER sing backup. Backup takes you out of the spotlight, and if you want to be a star, you should never be in the shadows. (Yes, I know I tell people backup is cool, but that's only because I don't want them to steal the attention I deserve!)

Tip #4

Read all of the gossip and celeb mags from front to back. That is the only way for you to be in on what's in and what's out. It's also a great way to figure out who's who and where the hot spot is to see or be seen.

Tip #3

Get noticed. And I don't mean in a tacky way, such as wearing skimpy clothes or dyeing your hair the same color as your crush's. Be subtle. You could, for example, go to every one of a certain Connect Three babe's classes, even if you already know everything there is to know.

Tip #2

If you have to, do whatever it takes to stop someone else from getting noticed. ESPECIALLY if that person is supertalented. (Like, you know, pretend you see a snake and start screaming).

Tip #1

And my number one tip if you are going to rock it to the top of the charts? It's simple. Like some wise person said: keep your friends close, and your enemies closer.

Bonus tip:
If you believe
something
will happen
hard enough,
it might
come true!

ELLA'S GUIDE TO DECORATING YOUR CABIN—VIBE STYLE!

Musical style doesn't have to be limited to your song choice or favorite instrument. It can be a part of your whole world—including your own room! Just check out some easy tips on how to transform your space from tone deaf to sweet harmony—just like my home away from home, the vibe cabin! ♡ _Ella

STENCILS!

Ask your parents if you can stencil some cool patterns on your walls or doors. Check out these patterns. Trace them onto cardboard and, voilà, stencils! If your parents won't let you do this, get a bulletin board and hang some stencils on there!

SET UP A STUDIO STATION!

Keep your computer, radio, portable music players, etc., all in one corner of your room. This can be your studio station—the place where you listen to music, download tunes, burn CDs, or even write your own songs.

Extra Stylin' Tidbit: If you want an authentic vibe cabin feel, grab a pine-scented candle!

28

POSTERS!

Hang lots of posters of your favorite musicians! That way, you can always have an eye on your favorite singer. Plus, it makes for some great inspiration.

PICTURE PERFECT!

Tape your pictures onto sheet-music paper or old CD covers to create a fun and funky border around your photos!

LYRIC MASTER

You know you have old song lyrics or favorite lines from a hot artist lying around. So don't waste them! Use magazines and papers to cut out the inspiring words and tape them to your walls. It will keep you thinking of music all day long.

And remember—pink is a very versatile color! Use your nail polish for inspiration!

KICK OUT THE JAMS!

There is one thing that the campers here don't do well—sit still. There is always something going on. And usually, it's a jam. That's when you can stand up and sing or dance or rhyme or prance. And Camp Rock doesn't just have jams—it has jams with attitude. Check it out!

CAMPFIRE JAM

My first jam of the summer! I was so nervous! Performing SOLO in front of all these kids? All these TALENTED kids? Not a fun thought! Being backup was a lot less nerve-racking!

Even Shane, ever-so cool and oh-so-famous, couldn't resist coming to the jam and checking out all the fresh talent!

PAJAMA JAM

Even though Tess, Ella, Peggy, and I agreed to wear matching outfits (in green, Shane's favorite color!) to Pajama Jam, Tess showed up in a totally different outfit. And it got worse! Caitlyn was totally doing her thing—and the crowd was way into it—until Tess distracted everyone by screaming!

I spent a lot of the summer getting ready to take the stage.

Even Shane was blown away by the talent at Camp Rock.

Caitlyn and I found some interesting—and unusual—places to practice.

30

FINAL JAM

Final Jam is the big one! The jam *everyone* wants to win. Which means—major drama, of course!

Tess was distracted, and totally stumbled during her performance. But one good thing happened—her mom, T.J. Tyler—was there to see the best part of her daughter's song!

Peggy, uh, Margaret Dupree, that is, completely wowed everyone and blew the crowd away with her performance. Connect Three was super impressed—they named her winner of Final Jam *and* of a duet recording with Shane!

And I finally got up the courage to sing a solo! It was awesome! (But not as awesome as singing with Shane!)

Peggy—aka Margaret—showed everyone her singing skills!

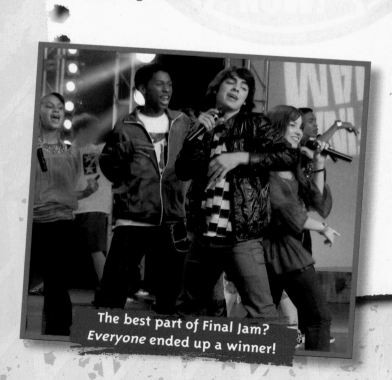

The best part of Final Jam? *Everyone* ended up a winner!

Sigh! This was definitely one of the highest notes of my summer!

CAMP ROCK MESSAGE

Pajama Jam

The biggest pajama party you'll ever attend! Grab your robe and slippers and get ready to ROCK!

Campfire Jam! Tonight!

Come on out and jam around the campfire! A Camp Rock experience NOT 2 B missed!

LOST AND FOUND

Lost—Totally Priceless (and by priceless, I mean worth more than your house!) Charm Bracelet. Last seen near kitchen. If found, call Tess's cell. If you're anyone, you have the digits.

Mystery Girl—Heard you singing and have been looking for you ever since. Where R U? UR voice is amazing. If U R My Mystery Girl, please meet me by the lake tonight.
—Shane

Shane—I'm the girl of your dreams. The voice! And I'm ready to connect with you!
—Dreaming of you

Shane—"Dreaming of you" is not the voice! I'm the voice. I'm the voice! I know it!!

CAMP ROCK
FIND YOUR OWN VOICE

Connie's Catering

Good Friends Deserve

Good Food

555-FOOD

BOARD

I can't believe they'll be performing here!!!

To whom it may concern:

I would like it known that food fights are so last year. Please try to control yourself. I ruined a perfectly good pair of shoes and my lawyer—well, my mother's lawyer—is going to hear about this. You know exactly who I am!

Looking for a drummer? Look no further! If you have a serious band that needs a serious drummer, text Andy. 555-1543

ROCK THE DAY AWAY WITH SHANE GRAY!

This is a total once-in-a-lifetime shot at being taught by a Camp Rock legend and a pop-star phenom! Don't miss out! Sign up for these classes ASAP—they WILL fill up fast!

Shane's Hip-Hop Dance Class
Wednesday @ 2 P.M.—Dance Studio

Shane's Stage Presence Class
Friday @ 10 A.M.—Lake Area Stage

Shane's Music 101 Class
Thursday @ 11 A.M.—Dance Studio

Final Jam

This is it—THE major event of the summer at Camp Rock. This year's top prize—the chance to record a track with Shane Gray of Connect Three! You do not want to miss it!

MUSICAL NOTES!

Hey Shane,

How's that birdhouse coming along? Think it will be ready the next time we come up for a visit?

Later,
Jason

Yo! Boys!

You gotta get me OUTTA here! I did my time — cold showers and all. I need civilization. I need hair gel. Although I did hear a girl singing the other day — AMAZING voice. Maybe I'll try to find my mystery girl while I wait for you guys to bail me out.

Later,
Shane

Greetings from

CAMP ROCK

Dear Sierra,

OMG, Camp Rock is so awesome! You would not believe the talent here. I am having the time of my life. And guess who's a celeb instructor here this summer? SHANE GRAY!
Can u believe it? Gotta go — time for kitchen duty!

See U Soon,
Mitchie

P.S. How do you say "sing it loud" in Mandarin?

QUAN.	DESCRIPTION							PRICE	AMOUNT

ADDRESS

CITY, STATE, ZIP

SOLD BY	CASH	C.O.D.	CHARGE	ON ACCT.	MDSE. RETD.	PAID OUT

1 Hi Mitchie,
2 So, how's my favorite rock star?
3 Mom says that you're making
4 lots of friends. But she hasn't
5 seen you take the stage for
6 a solo yet. What gives? I'll see
7 you at Final Jam!
8
9 Love,
10 Dad
11
12 P.S. Sorry for the odd paper—
13 Not much choice at a hardware
14 store!

TAX

TOTAL

Mitchie—
kitchen duty—
NOW!

See! Camp Rock
is not all fun! :(

Hi Mother,

It's me, Tess. I haven't heard
from you but saw your picture
in Star Scoop. The tour
looks like it's going well.
Just wondering if you will
be coming to Camp Rock for
Final Jam. No biggie, really.
Just wondering. If not, I'll
see you in a few weeks.

Toodles,
Tess

Hi Mom,
I need a few things
in my next care
package, OK? Please
send sparkly pink lip
gloss, clear lip gloss,
strawberry lip gloss,
cherry lip gloss, banana
lip gloss, sparkly clear
lip gloss, powder pink
nail polish, perfectly
pink nail polish, and
power pink nail polish?
OK?

LUV U LOTS,
Ella

Mom—

I need a new battery for
my laptop.
Oh, and Tess is up to her
old tricks, and I think she
found a new pet named
Mitchie.

Later!
Caitlyn

BE TRUE TO YOU:

Everything I needed to learn, I learned at Camp Rock. By Mitchie Torres

Take it from me—the best way to live your life is to be true to you! I know from experience that the glitz and glamour of someone else's life might seem really cool, but if you have to give up everything that you are, it's SO not worth it. After the summer I had, there are a few things I just HAVE to share.

DON'T be blinded by the popular crowd. Just because they're popular does not mean that they have a better life than you. That old cliché, appearances can be deceiving? That is a cliché for a reason—it's true!

DO hang out with the people you feel most comfortable with. There's a reason you feel comfortable—these are probably the people you have the most in common with. That means they are the ones most likely to have your back when you need them.

DO tell the truth about yourself. No matter what, there is nothing to be ashamed of. Everyone leads a different life and has different advantages and disadvantages. It's never cool to lie about who you are. It only leads to trouble! (Believe me!)

DON'T do things that don't feel right to you. If you want to sing lead, take the mike! You know your talents—showcase 'em!

DO take your own advice. If you tell someone you care about that they should be true to themselves, then that advice is worth taking yourself. You wouldn't give a friend bad advice, right?

DO be proud of who you are and where you come from. After all, it's what made you the person you are today.

DON'T get pressured into doing, saying, or wearing things that you just don't want to. Individuals rock!

DO have the courage to beat your own drum and do what you love. You'll have a good time, and it will show!

FOLLOW YOUR DREAM

DON'T ever do anything stupid or silly or humiliating in the name of being someone you're not—even if you think that new someone is a better version of who you really are. Take it from me, the REAL YOU rocks— even if the real you is a total klutz!

MITCHIE AND SHANE: CAMP ROCK DREAM DUET

Of course, as soon as he was spotted on the Camp Rock grounds, Shane was chased by screaming girls! A member of Connect Three—in the flesh!—it was too great! To escape, he hid behind a bush. While there, he heard a girl singing. He loved the song and loved the girl's voice even more! He spent the whole summer searching for his mystery girl. Turns out, it was me!

Our road to friendship was NOT smooth. Not only was Shane rockin' a spoiled attitude, I was pretending to be someone I wasn't. Talk about a bad foundation for trust! But after a few bumps—like

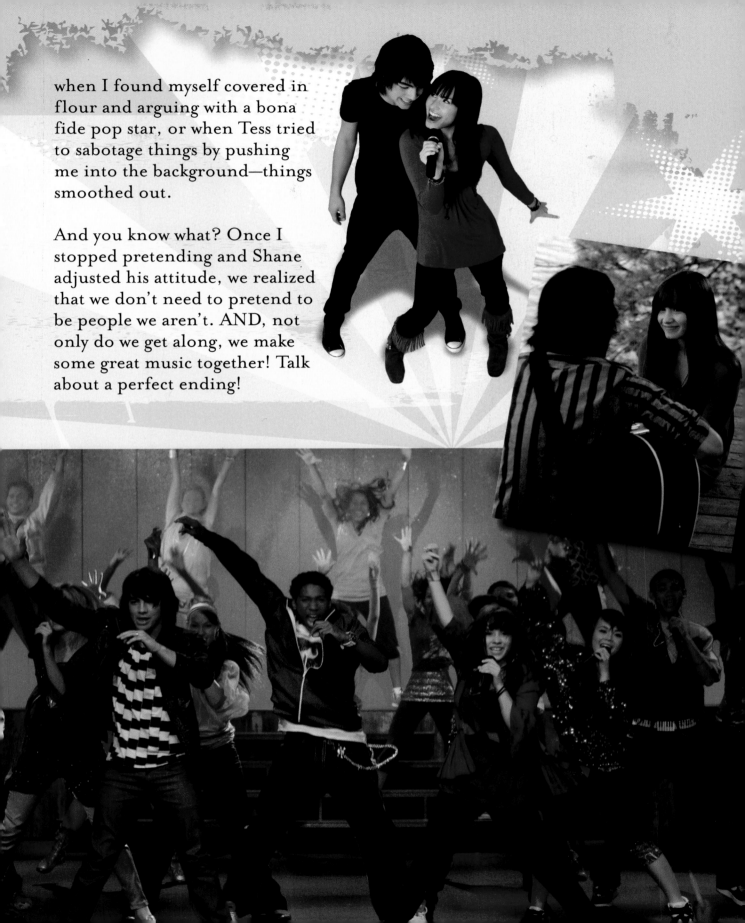

when I found myself covered in flour and arguing with a bona fide pop star, or when Tess tried to sabotage things by pushing me into the background—things smoothed out.

And you know what? Once I stopped pretending and Shane adjusted his attitude, we realized that we don't need to pretend to be people we aren't. AND, not only do we get along, we make some great music together! Talk about a perfect ending!

MITCHIE'S SONGBOOK PART 2

Now that I have had this awesome experience at Camp Rock, my songbook is packed with stuff! So much inspiration for a ton of new songs. Here are some pages from the end of camp . . . a change from what was in my journal when I first arrived, huh?

Tess found out my mom doesn't work for Hot Tunes. And she told everyone! Now everyone knows who I really am. At first I was mortified. But now that Caitlyn's come around, I am starting to feel a little bit better.

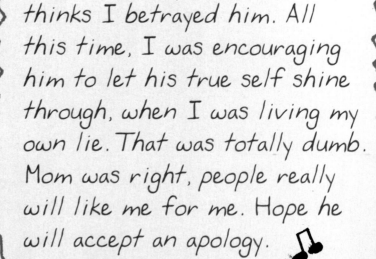

Shane is really mad at me. He thinks I betrayed him. All this time, I was encouraging him to let his true self shine through, when I was living my own lie. That was totally dumb. Mom was right, people really will like me for me. Hope he will accept an apology.

Tess lied! She claims Caitlyn and I stole her charm bracelet! Brown has banned us from performing until AFTER Final Jam. But I might have a plan. . . .

Final Jam was absolutely amazing. Even if I didn't win (Peggy SO deserved it, anyway), it was my moment to shine. And Shane was right there to share the best moment of my life. Total perfection!

I feel like I, the REAL Mitchie Torres, can do anything! Camp Rock rules!

mitchie

K.I.T.
(Keep in Touch)

I made some great music—and friends— this summer. Check out what they had to say!
    —Mitchie

To My Mystery Girl,
I am SO glad that I met you this summer and that YOU are the one who turned out to be my mystery girl! I hope now that I found you, I don't lose you again!
Shane

Hey Mitchie,
You are a totally cool girl—just wish you'd realized that a lot sooner and been yourself from the beginning! well, better late than never! E-mail me when you get home. Hopefully, you can come visit me really soon! Talk to you later,
Caitlyn

Dearest Mitchie,
Can't say that bunking with you was the highlight of my summer. After all, I live with the most awesome person ever—ME! But I guess I'm sorry that things got out of hand at the end. You have a pretty OK voice, I guess, and I shouldn't have framed you. If you make it to Camp Rock next session, I guess I'll C U then.
Toodles,
Tess Tyler

Keep On Jammin'. Girl!
C U Next Session!
--Barron

Hi Mitchie,
I had so much fun this session. Hope you did, too. I think you should get some peach lip gloss—it's such a pretty color!
Bye-Bye,
Ella

Dear Mitchie,
I'm glad you came to camp this summer. I think we are going to become great friends—especially now that we'll both be spending so much time with Shane!
All the best,
Peggy

B True 2 U 4Eva!
—Sander

We'll rock it out again next session! If you ever want to get a backstage Broadway pass, call me! K.I.T.
—Lola

Find your rhythm!
—Andy

CAMP ROCK

CAMP ROCK JAMMIES

Welcome to the Camp Rock Jammies—the awards I would give to honor the best of the best at Camp Rock! This session has been pretty intense, with some major talent. Which means—fierce competition in some of the categories, mates! Check out the winners!

—Brown

Brown made Camp Rock so much fun! It's cool to see what he thought, but I couldn't help adding my own comments. :)

—M

Hottest Male Performer
And the Jammy Goes to . . .
SHANE!

Duh! Did we have a doubt?!?

Most Promising Future Performer
And the Jammy Goes to . . .
MITCHIE!
No pressure!!

Soul Singer of the Summer

And the Jammy Goes to . . .

LOLA!

Next stop...
Broadway!

Best Breakout Performance

And the Jammy Goes to . . .

PEggY!

Or, should we say Margaret!

Producer of the Future

And the Jammy Goes to . . .

CAITLYN!

She hears the sound of the future!

Drummer of the Summer

And the Jammy Goes to . . .

Beware the **ANDY!** drumsticks!

Best Backup Singer

And the Jammy Goes to . . .

ELLA!

It's all about the lip gloss!

Hip-Hop Honors

And the Jammy Goes to . . .

BARRON and SANDER!

These boys really stepped it up!

Diva with the Most 'Tude

And the Jammy Goes to . . .

TESS!

Some people never change!

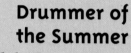

A CAMP ROCK SUMMER TO REMEMBER!

In the Kitchen with Mom

Connect Three

The Famous Tortilla-Chip Incident

New Beginnings

Tess Tyler Knows How to Stay Connected.

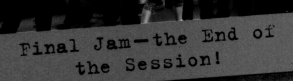

Final Jam—the End of the Session!